War Kids
1941 – 1945

WW II Through the
Eyes of Children

Lloyd Hornbostel

1996
Galde Press, Inc.
Lakeville, Minnesota

War Kids.

First Edition
First Printing, 1996

Cover art and interior illustrations by Charles Scogins

Library of Congress Cataloging-in-Publication Data

Hornbostel, Lloyd, 1934–
    War kids, 1941–1945 : WW II through the eyes of children \
Lloyd Hornbostel. — 1st ed.
        p.   cm.
    ISBN 1–880090–27–9 (trade pbk.)
        1. World War, 1939–1945—United States—Fiction
    2. Community life—United States—Fiction.   3. Children—
    United States—Fiction.   4. War stories, American. I. Title.
    PS3558.068726W3   1995
    813'.54—dc20   95–41236
                                                                           CIP

Galde Press, Inc.
PO Box 460
Lakeville, Minnesota 55044

Dedication

To those fathers and mothers
who made the supreme sacrifice
so that their children could grow
up in a free and secure America.

Contents

Prologue

Our human existence has never been completely free of conflict. Wars are waged for all sorts of reasons, and World War II has its own set. While much has been written about the adult experience, little has been concerned with the lives of the children of a war. War kids is their view—kids growing up during World War II.

Fathers went off to fight, mothers to the factories, and kids were left with a mix of adult chores, and a special kind of recreation that was never fully separated from war times.

Toys were lacking (metal was needed for tanks and airplanes), and the loss of adult contact created play schemes unique to the times. Play was also a necessary release from the fear of the conflict. Often, the ringing of the phone, or a letter in the mail brought home the real tragedy of war. Kids were drawn into the war along with everyone else.

The collection of incidents which make up this book are written from a child's view and understanding of World War II. Their laughter and sorrow reflect the moods of a small mid-American community. I hope that you will enjoy them, perhaps with a bit of nostalgia, or simply as stories.

1

Fords and Families

Nobody seemed to know much about electricity. They sure were using a lot of that stuff in the war—radar—man, you could see them planes miles off. Gosh!

Miss Thomas wasn't much help—not that she wasn't a good teacher—but I don't think she knew electricity. She'd just tell us to stay away from the stuff.

Ole man Anderson lived across the street in one of those big, white wood frame houses built when trees were almost free. I never knew what Anderson did. He never talked to kids and acquired a limp shortly after they started up the draft.

Anderson liked Fords. He had two or three of them in a stable back of the house. That stable was full of all kinds of junk; I would have given anything to get inside. Anderson didn't talk to us, or anyone else for that matter. None of us wanted to try him. Only time I heard him talk was when he worked on his Fords. He talked a real lot one time when the emergency brake on one of his Fords let go and took off hell bent in high gear. Didn't stop till it hit the stable door. Anderson talked a lot about the Lord when he worked on those Fords. I thought for a time he was a minister, but Ma just said that folks who own Fords always talk that way.

Ole man Anderson didn't know it, but he started my career in electricity one day when working on a Ford. One of the coils bit him and he chucked the spark coil in the hedgerow. He sure gave the Lord a real dressing that day.

Anderson's old lady sent him packing to the post office that afternoon, and it was then that I decided to look for that coil. I knew it had something to do with electricity the way Anderson let go of it. There it was—just where he'd chucked it. That coil sure looked impressive with the varnished wood and all them springs and buttons. I stuffed it under my shirt and stole for home.

Hack was a good kind of friend—willing—just the right amount of brains not to be a problem. My pa and his dad were on some island in the Pacific. We knew to leave our mothers alone when the mail came. Hack had one other real virtue; he collected books. One was an owner's manual for a Model T Ford. The other item

Hack had when he arrived with his wagon was a battery from his dad's car. His mom didn't drive so the car was blocked up. Hack had studied every part of that car from the V-8 motor to the oil brakes. Someday Hack would be something big—he was that kind. There were some wires in the wagon and something I didn't understand—Hack called it a voltmeter.

Pa's work bench ran along one side of the garage. Ma almost never went out there. I think it reminded her of Pa.

Hack spent a long time reading the Ford manual, and every once in a while he'd ask me to attach a wire here and there. The last wire he connected himself, and that wood coil started to buzz just like Anderson's Ford before he cranked it. Hack's expression told me that we were in the electrical age.

Ma had a clothes wire strung from the back porch to the garage. It was just a dumb clothes wire to me, but to Hack it looked like those radio wires we kept seeing in the newsreel shorts. He connected a wire from the coil to the hook where the clothes wire was attached to the garage.

The experiment would have ended there except for divine providence intervening in the form of Mrs. Wilson. Neither Hack nor I liked Mrs. Wilson—she was one of those front-row church people who never did anything wrong—or anything for that matter. She did have a nice flower garden and on occasion would bring a basket of cuttings over to Ma. The course of history was changed that day when, while we had the clothes wire hooked to the Ford coil, Mrs. Wilson decided to bring some flowers to my ma, and finding my ma out, hung (or tried to) the basket on the clothes wire.

We never found the flowers, but managed to locate the basket. It ended up on the garage roof when Mrs. Wilson "completed the circuit," to use Hack's terms. I never knew somebody Mrs. Wilson's age could move that fast, either. It was also the first time I heard Mrs. Wilson talk about the Lord outside of church.

2

The Electronic
Outhouse

I would have been more than satisfied with that one unique demonstration in electrical energy transmission, but Hack was a true pioneer. In future years, that same mind would be exploring the fringes of semiconductor technology, but today Hack had an idea for the ultimate demonstration.

Hack's family lived on the edge of town. They didn't farm, but grew enough vegetables to keep them through the winter. I loved the smell of that huge pot of fresh tomatoes stewing just before Hack's mom ladled jars full and waxed them tight for the winter.

Hack's mom was like Hack—she never looked like she was working till you tried to keep up with her. Hack got his knowledge from his mom, too. There was nothing that she couldn't fix or run around the place. A single crank on the Graverly or a flip of the flywheel on the old Fairbanks "Z" engine, and things moved. My ma didn't even know what a flywheel was!

Hack's family also had an outhouse, and for some reason his genius centered on this artifact. Ma did not allow "outhouse jokes" in my family, but Hack had a mental library on the subject. I could almost hear his mind at work as we pushed our bikes up the lane to the Grange Hall.

With the war effort, new farm machinery was non-existent in our parts. You made do with what you had when the war broke out. There were even a few steam rigs still working separators; the bombers needed the gasoline more than we did. The Grange, in an effort to keep the farms operating, held a huge sale every spring where most anything could be bought, sold, and traded. The auctioneer's song joined the sounds of spring winds on new leaves, and the birds, back for another season in their eternal cycle. The war was remote, far off except for those stars on the honor roll. There would be no more springs or Grange auctions for those names beside the stars.

Hack was ahead of me now—almost to the Grange Hall outhouse. We quickly attached two wires to the structure, one to the old tin sheet that covered the rotting floor and the other to the eave trough nailed to the wall. I stopped to read some of the poetic humor carved in the wall, but Hack was impatient as usual. I looked back for a moment as we closed the

gate. The flag was at half mast on the pole. Soon there would be a fresh mound of soil on the hill, and another star on the bronze plate.

Auction day was jammed with people from the farms. You could tell the city folk—they smelled different. No one noticed two boys pulling a wagon covered with an old throw rug. No one seemed to think that it was a strange place to leave a wagon—behind the outhouse.

Hack was also a collector—whatever he made from his paper route he saved for the auction. It was his day. Hack would touch something nondescript and call it by name. "Armature"—"rod"—"magneto," meant little to me, but to Hack they were the makings of an education. He would pause just long enough to explain their function to me. I would nod whether I understood or not and we would move on to another treasure.

Mid-afternoon saw the outhouse busy. Lunch and the beer tent were producing the desired result. I was to learn that Hack's schemes, simple as they were, were not always foolproof. Hack positioned himself by the corner of the Grange Hall where he could signal me as I sat behind the outhouse. I would wait a respectable time for our customer to become situated, and then I was to make the vital connection to the coil and battery. The only flaw in our plan is that we'd failed to agree on a signal.

I saw Hack raise his arm in a frantic wave, and then he motioned again to me and started to run away from the Grange Hall. While I was trying to figure out what Hack was up to, I heard sounds of activity in the outhouse. Almost without thinking, I attached the coil wire to the battery.

Remember those warhoops at the charge in the cowboy-Indian movies? Well, what came out of that outhouse was ten times louder than anything any Indian hollered on the screen. Hack heard it too, and he picked up speed; I was already in a dead run. I don't know how far we ran, but I could hear peals of laughter behind me. Had we turned to watch, we would have seen the local sheriff running, or at least attempting to run as best a man can with his pants down to his ankles.

It was a long afternoon under Hallsey's corncrib, but it gave Hack and I some time to reflect on experimental electronics. He finally asked me if I had seen who it was that made the "connection" in the outhouse. When he told me that it was the sheriff, I felt the ground grow wet beneath my stomach. I bought my wagon back the next year for twenty-five cents. The election that fall gave us a new sheriff, and the Grange installed indoor plumbing. An old piece of tin, half buried in the ground, was the only monument remaining to one of man's most noble experiments.

3

Carbs and Growing Up

Ma was at me again on how we were always playing and not doing anything for "the effort." I guess she was right, only I didn't want to admit to it. Still, there was not too much we could do—like working in a factory building bombs or something else neat like that. Ma had heard all of my excuses before; she'd lay off for a bit, but the subject would return.

We had one of the best softball teams in town—more because of our size than our skill. Our pitcher, Andy Kessmer, was one of the coolest shots I've ever seen. Nothing rattled him—or at least it seemed that way. He never talked much either, so it was unusual when he stayed around after our game with Milford. Milford, by the way, never got a hit off Andy.

Andy's dad owned a small machine shop—one of those places that did everything. I'd never been inside the place, but the outside was littered with farm machinery and wood crates of parts all waiting to be fixed or machined. We never talked too much about the war; Andy's brother went down with the *Arizona*.

Anyway, as I was saying, it was unusual for Andy to stick around. He was pretty direct—they needed some help at the shop. My visions of building bombs single-handed evaporated, but some work would get Ma off my back.

It was pretty dark inside the shop as Andy's dad led us to a small back room filled with wood crates and a few chairs mixed around an oak table. A calendar hung on the wall displaying most of "Miss Torque Wrench." An old wood icebox under the calendar displayed another photo and cautioned entrants to pay for their beer. We were in the poker room.

Our job was really simple—Andy's dad had a government contract to assemble P-40 carbs and we had to unpack all of the parts, clean them in fuel oil, and place each part in a tote bin. It was pretty dull stuff, and we rotated the jobs so that we got some relief. At least when Hack and I went home, we could say with some honesty that we were now part of the "effort."

Hack, as usual, had to know how the thing worked, and Andy's dad was sure nice to take the time to show us a finished carb and explain it to us. We left it in the center of the poker table along with a

photo of the aircraft. Somewhere out over the Pacific they were relying on us.

It was my turn at the carb floats, as they were called by Andy's dad. I dumped a lot into the kerosene tank and used an old canoe paddle to force them beneath the surface. Only this afternoon something was different. Some of the floats stayed submerged. Hack pulled one out and watched the kerosene leak from the seam. Someone had forgotten to apply solder to make the float airtight.

Andy's dad was pretty upset about the whole thing, and while he was on the telephone with some government inspector, we had to test every float by holding it submerged for what seemed hours and then shaking it to see if any fuel oil leaked into the interior. I guess I didn't think it was much of a problem until six Army Air Force officers greeted us one morning the following week. I knew that they were important because the poker room was cleaned, Miss Torque Wrench had disappeared, and a file cabinet had replaced the icebox. We even had new folding chairs.

I never said "sir" so many times in my life as I did that day. Hack and I showed how we discovered the problem, and our test to check for other bad floats. We all had to sign a whole bunch of papers and swear not to talk to anyone about the problem. That night I went to bed without supper—sleep wouldn't come either; I kept thinking about some aviator out there heading off a swarm of Japs, and that carb float not working.

I remember we loaded up all those parts into an Army truck, and almost a week later we got new floats. We were pretty quiet in the poker room. I'd started to forget the thing when, late one afternoon, Andy's dad called us up to the front office. On his desk was a letter of commendation from the Secretary of the Army for "quick action" that had probably saved the lives of many of our fighting men. Our names were in there too. His dad watched us as we each read the letter. Then he got up slowly, shook our hands with a feel that I will never forget, and walked over to the wall where a photo of Andy's brother hung. He placed the letter beneath the photo, and I turned so the others wouldn't see my tears.

Today Andy runs that shop—they employ hundreds of people now. In the lobby is a photo of a handsome young aviator and, alongside it, a letter.

4

Ma's Victory Garden and the Great Organic Fertilizer Experiment

That infantry soldier who dug his way across North Africa and Europe got his start in a victory garden for certain. Dig up the ground in the spring, dig weeds all summer, and dig up the vegetables in the fall. But those gardens were part of our life, and not only for the food. If you wanted social status in our town, a victory garden was the way up. The bigger the better, and the annual civic garden award? Well, if you won that prize, you were untouchable. I know Ma dreamed of that honor, but it required a labor of love, and love did not exactly fit our own thoughts concerning victory gardens. It was our duty, though, to slave on.

Our yard soil wouldn't have produced a peanut save for generous applications of fertilizer. We got

ours from Collier's stables every spring when they
cleaned the stalls. We'd stand knee deep in that stuff,
spreading it across the topsoil, and spading the mess
to cut some of the smell. The whole operation took
one good weekend out of baseball season.

The first hint of trouble came when Mr. Collier
called Ma and said since he'd lost the dairy wagon
contract last fall his team had been in the field. He had
only enough fertilizer for his own garden. Ma sent us
packing for new fertilizer horizons.

I should have been suspicious when Hack and I,
returning from fishing one afternoon, noticed a sign
on the Grange bulletin board offering free "organic
compost." It said to contact Nelson's hog farm. We
got our bikes and headed out to west-end corners
where Nelson ran his farm along with the general
store, post office, and tavern. Nelson was most always
in the tavern.

He seemed nice enough, but a little hard to understand. Nelson spat part of a plug while telling us the
merits of liquid pig manure and how to ditch the garden for this advanced form of fertilizer. He had a tank
wagon and let the stuff run out on your garden. No
spreading—no spade work, it was too good to be
true. It was!

Well, anyway, Hack and I built up a berm of dirt
all around our garden just as Nelson had told us to
do. Ma didn't take much notice of our work. I think
she was glad that we'd found Nelson's supply.

Nelson pulled up late that afternoon with a giant
tank wagon behind his tractor. There wasn't much to

it. He connected an old section of fire hose to the bottom of the tank and opened a valve.

As he left, we looked at a shimmering pool of foul-smelling brown slime where our garden had been. Ma closed the windows on that side of the house and we avoided discussing the matter during supper. I woke up during the night to the sound of thunder. One of those brief spring storms was rolling across the plain. The steady downpour of the rain sent me off to sleep again with its musical clatter on our tin garage roof. Outside, a crack was appearing in one corner of our berm. We had not designed our fortification for two inches of rain.

I don't know what got me up that morning—the smell, or all those voices. Looking out my window, I observed a brown sea flowing from our garden down the drive and up against the side of Mrs. Wilson's house. About that time her basement window gave way. I could barely make out the outline of Mrs. Wilson's face in the window before the tide engulfed her.

Well, that year we had the greenest side yard (so did Mrs. Wilson), and Ma got a blue ribbon for the highest yield of any garden in the city. Mrs. Wilson never brought Ma any more cut flowers, though.

5

We're Introduced to Culture and Other Forms

I always thought culture was something you were born with—kids with culture dressed different, and did different things. We weren't snobs—it was just that we did our lives in our way and somehow culture had to be injected. Like getting a shot—it hurt initially, but you got over it.

Then there was the LaRose family. They had culture but it didn't show. Marco was the only friend I had who could field a ball while whistling Bach. His sister, Angelica, also crossed over to our side. She was a girl, and could look like a girl when she dressed up for Sunday. Angelica played with us and, even though we watched our language and where we went to the bathroom, she was one of us. Ma said Angelica would be a movie star when she grew up—Ma was right—but right now we counted on her for stealing bases.

Miss O'Neil taught dance, and she was also a friend of Angelica's. Ma knew Miss O'Neil because they were both in the war relief knitting club. Miss O'Neil also had culture. One time she danced for our school assembly, and anyone who could run around on her toes like that had to have culture.

Anyway, one afternoon I was walking home with Angelica after a baseball game where she'd pulled the game out for us with three stolen bases. She was unusually quiet. I guess we walked for a couple of blocks in silence when she told me that her oldest brother was missing in action. She spoke as if she had to tell someone, and I muttered some response, but Angelica understood. It was another one of those strange moments when the war was very close.

We stopped for a minute at the town square, and in a very quiet voice Angelica asked me if I would take dancing lessons with her. If my ma had asked me that question, my answer would have sent me to bed early. Maybe it was the mood—or Angelica—but I heard myself reply in the affirmative. For a second Angelica took my hand and squeezed it. I walked home trying to figure out why I didn't mind being handled by a girl.

When the word got out, I wasn't too popular with Hack and Andy. Their mothers used me as a wedge to get them to enroll in Miss O'Neil's class. Still, they were pretty nice about it, more out of respect for Angelica than for me.

The old mill ballroom was built during the 1920s. Ma said that all the big bands had played there one time or the other. The bands, or what was left of them, were overseas now, with the troops. Paint peeled from the wood latticework, and there were water stains on the maple floor where the roof leaked. A basketball hoop had been installed at one end of the floor. The only music at the mill ballroom now came from Miss O'Neil's creaky Victrola.

Miss O'Neil would show each of us a step, and then we would dance with each other. She would count out the beat, repeating the instructions for each step. It really wasn't all that bad. I didn't know why Angelica took the course, though—she danced like she was floating off the floor. Two things scared me— I was getting to like dancing, and especially dancing with Angelica.

Miss O'Neil always gave us a break during the lessons, and Hack and I were sitting on the edge of the dam throwing stones into the mill pond. We were pretending that the floating leaves were enemy ships and our stones "bombs." I heard Hack let out a yell behind me as he was searching for more ammunition, and turned to see him proudly displaying a bull snake. Hack loved wildlife, especially snakes, and a bull snake was a real prize. It was a beauty, and I knew Hack would keep it. I watched him stuff the reptile in his shirt as Miss O'Neil called us back inside.

I'd half forgotten that snake till Miss O'Neil called on Hack to demonstrate the foxtrot with her. Glen

Miller started out at full crank and, as I danced with Angelica, I half followed Hack locked in combat with Miss O'Neil. Hack was born with three feet, and the foxtrot required only two.

It all happened so fast that I really didn't see much except that Miss O'Neil let out the loudest yell I've ever heard come out of a woman and then headed straight for the outhouse. Hack just stood there, frozen in place, while his bull snake slithered across the floor and disappeared in the latticework. I could feel Angelica shaking in my arms—she was laughing! It didn't take her long to regain her composure, and to follow Miss O'Neil to the outhouse.

Angelica and I walked back to town and I waited in front of Miss O'Neil's house while Angelica procured a change of clothing for our instructor. When that bull snake had poked its head out of Hack's shirt and started to slither up Miss O'Neil's arm, that was too much.

Hack stayed in our class, but Miss O'Neil never danced with him again. With him, culture was at best a truce.

6

Bill

The first week of the fall school term had not gotten off to a good start. This was the subject of the conversation between Hack and myself as we walked home after our football practice. The initial blow came when we were told that our principal, Mr. Johnson, had been drafted and would not be returning to our school. He had been classified as 4F, but when he took a second physical, what was wrong with him seemed to have gone away. I thought of him getting yelled at by some drill sergeant instead of yelling at us. Worse, the rumor was that his replacement was to be a retired woman kindergarten teacher. The final blow came at football practice when our coach told us that he was being transferred from the

instrument company where he worked as an inspector. Ma worked there too, and she gave Mr. Stang
much credit for their getting the Army Navy E for
zero rejects last year. This was our first year to play
tackle football instead of touch, but the chances of
making that change without a coach were nil.

We had been silent for a few minutes, and maybe
that was why I felt that something was following us.
I stopped, turned, and saw what appeared to be a dog
about halfway down the block. The dog stopped and
sat down, not wanting to come any closer. We contin-
ued our walk to the next corner, where Hack turned
to go to his house, and I again saw the dog, only by
now he had come within some fifty feet of us. Obvi-
ously a stray, the poor animal looked half starved
even from that distance. We had seen strays before
when some families disrupted by the war had let their
pets loose to roam the streets.

I made my way the last two blocks to our house,
stopping on the porch to see if the dog was still following. It was still there and now had lain down on the
sidewalk just below the porch steps. The dog was a
male with short hair all matted with burrs, but it was
his eyes that made me stare at him. They seemed to
show all of the suffering he had been through, yet they
had a sparkle of hope that I might be the one who
would call him friend. For some reason, I called him
Bill, and he walked slowly to my feet. Bill had arrived.

I knew Ma would be late Friday because that was
the day all the bombsights were inspected. Everyone

stayed until all of the production had been accepted
and packed for shipment. Bill and I had been on our
porch for the better part of two hours by the time Ma
arrived. I had picked the burrs from his coat and fed
him a number of bowls of milk and corn flakes. I had
also been making up all the reasons why I should be
allowed to keep Bill. After all, Pa had kept a hunting
dog before the war. It was a purebred bird hunter
which had cost Pa a small fortune, according to Ma.
The dog went to a farm when Pa enlisted.

Bill was anything but a purebreed, with a mixture
of beagle, foxhound, terrier, and probably a little lab
influence. His coat seemed to be mostly black and tan
with a white saddle. I had tried to give him a bath
with a wet dishcloth so that he would look a little better for Ma.

When Ma arrived, I was sitting with Bill lying on
my old gym jacket. I was about to launch into my list
when Ma and Bill met eye to eye. Ma was no match for
that helpless gaze and remarked almost as an after-
thought that I should take the dog to see Doctor Armstrong tomorrow. I decided to say nothing and take the
acceptance of Bill into our home one day at a time. I left
him that night on the porch, wrapped in the coat.

Next morning I rushed downstairs even though it
was Saturday to see if Bill was still where I had left
him. I received a wag of his tail and a lick on the side
of my face when I unwrapped him. We took a long
walk, and he would come to my side at the mere mention of his new name. Pa's bird dog never was that

well trained even after obedience school. I gave him another three bowls of cereal for breakfast, which seemed to satisfy him. I left Bill on the porch while I ate inside, but when Ma left for the store I opened the porch door and let him inside.

Bill was not used to being inside a house, and his first attempt to climb the stairs up to my room ended in a pile of dog back down on the living room floor. I carried him upstairs and let him wander while I finished dressing. When I returned from the bathroom, Bill was firmly placed on my bed at the foot. It was to become his sleeping space for the rest of his life.

I had never had any experience with house training a dog, but either Bill had previous training or was anxious to please me. We never had a mistake.

Doctor Armstrong was neither a doctor or vet; there were many stories about his past and few went to him for medical problems. He did have a way with animals which came in handy when our real vet was called to serve in the K-9 Corps. He and Doctor Armstrong were friends of a sort, and I had seen a postcard from our vet with a picture of some Alaskan sled dogs on the front taped to his office window. I found an old collar from Pa's dog and walked Bill downtown on a leash. The restraint was probably not necessary, but I did not want to take any chances. We walked around the park so Bill would be emptied out before his vet experience. He received two shots along with a tag for his collar. The doctor said that Bill was about one year old and, other than being thin for lack of food, was in good shape. I was told to feed him and love him, something I never forgot to do. On the way home, I picked up a bag of dog ration at the feed mill. Bill thus far had cost me two dollars and eighty cents out of my paper route profits.

When I got home, I asked Ma to let Bill inside with the excuse that I was going to give him a bath. The scam worked, because that night a very clean dog slept on the foot of my bed. I placed my gym jacket there so Ma would not get on me about dog hair on my sheets.

Training Bill was a joint venture, because we both had to get to know each other along with what my commands meant. Bill was smart: two repeats of a command, and he had it in his mind.

He had one bad habit which I found out about on the way home from the visit to the vet. Bill liked to chase cats. I had made the mistake of stopping by to show Bill to Angelica, who happened to be on their porch swing holding the family angora cat. Bill cleared the porch steps in one leap and, after a brief skirmish, the cat retreated to the top of a power pole in the front yard. It did not seem to be the right time to visit with Angelica, and after apologies, Bill and I set out for home.

Bill was a welcome addition to an otherwise slow school year. We never did get a new football coach and, after one game attempted without one, our new principal cancelled the season. One look at her and I was sure that in her younger years she could have played football herself.

Bill followed me everywhere, including school. I carried the old gym jacket and put it in the outer coat room so that he could have a place of shelter from the weather. Recess found him indulging in another favorite sport—catching baseballs. I think the retriever in him took over, and Bill could field batting practice balls for hours. He had a way of catching the ball sideways in his mouth so as to absorb the impact while not damaging the ball.

His skill actually benefited a cause when, during one of our games with our west side school, bets were made as to how many balls Bill would catch during the seventh inning stretch. Proceeds were to go to the Red Cross War Relief Fund, and Bill was dressed in a K-9 Red Cross coat such as was used on the battlefield. Bets went up to fifty balls, a number which he had never achieved, but I was confident that some of the smaller bets would be made. I went out in the outfield with him, giving Bill a small meat scrap as a treat. We talked boy to dog for a minute while the batter was warming up. That day Bill made over two hundred dollars for the Red Cross, and after his fifty-first continuous catch, he received a standing ovation from the crowd. I could tell that his mouth was sore and his gums were bleeding a little, so he spent the remainder of the game on my lap consuming a chocolate ice cream shake for strictly medical purposes.

Perhaps Bill's most famous feat came quite by accident. I would always let him out at night after the ten o'clock war news. Though Ma never told me, I knew that Pa had some sort of a code worked up in his letters so that she knew about where he was. Ma always kept his most recent letters handy so that she could compare Pa's messages with the radio announcements. Bill knew to wait until the broadcast was over before he made his evening trip over to the porch door. This was the only time that I would let him out alone, because he seemed to want a little private time, perhaps to relive for a moment his days of vagabond freedom. I always felt that Bill was not completely domesticated in our ways. He would return in about an hour and scratch at the door to be let in for the night. Summer and winter, it was the same routine with him.

I remember it being late May, because we were watching the gradual invasion of Germany. Pa was somewhere in the middle of all of it, and Ma knew where. Bill went to the door and I let him out as usual. It was a Wednesday. Bill was gone for almost two hours, and just as I was beginning to worry about him, I heard the familiar scratch at the porch door. Bill came in and dropped a large white package at my feet. He was treating whatever it was as a special gift, so I praised him for his effort. I picked up the package—it was heavy and freezing cold, which did not make any sense for a warm spring night. I handed the thing to Ma.

The next thing I knew, Ma let out a warhoop like she had been shot and poor Bill made for under the dining room table. On the kitchen counter lay the largest T-bone steak that I had ever seen. It was frozen for the most part, with a few teeth marks from being transported by Bill. It would have taken a month of meat stamps to buy that piece of meat, and no butcher shop in our town ever had cuts of meat that size.

Ma placed the meat in the refrigerator, more out of not knowing what else to do with it. I know she was tempted to serve it to us for a meal despite its unknown origin and the fact that it had been in Bill's mouth. There was no reason to ask any of our friends if the meat had been taken from them: that cut was far beyond the means of anyone we knew. I decided not to say anything about the incident to my friends. I don't know for certain, but frugality eventually got the best of Ma, and I think we saw a lot of that steak as hamburger casserole dishes.

Bill did nothing unusual for the next few days, and I forgot about the incident. School was coming to a close, resulting in little activity except for studying for tests. One good thing did happen during the school year: our aged principal suffered chest pains in January after trying to break up an interschool snowball fight, and was replaced by another woman who was younger, along with being an expert tennis coach. She even got a few of us boys to take up the sport.

I had forgotten the following Wednesday that this was the day of the week that Bill had caught the steak, so I let him out as usual that night. Once again he was almost an hour late, and I almost expected to see him return with more meat. He did not disappoint us; his next prize was a giant porterhouse wrapped in the same white paper. At this rate, we would be eating like kings—except that those steaks belonged to someone and our dog was stealing them. I decided to confide in Hack about the whole affair the next day. At first I don't think that he believed me, but when I showed him Bill's last catch in the refrigerator, he stopped giving me a hard time.

During test time, there was not much time to think about dogs and mystery meat, but I was determined to somehow follow Bill the next Wednesday to find the source of his misdeeds.

That following Wednesday morning, I told Hack my plan. We would ditch our bicycles in back of our garage so our mothers would not hear us getting them out of the shed. We probably would be able to keep up with Bill, and if it was a clear night there would be enough moonlight to track him. I would bring Pa's flashlight from his car so we would have one way to spot Bill if we lost him. Ma had war relief knitting along with Hack's mom, so we would be free to be out for about an hour before they returned. The only question was if Bill would repeat his strange activity for a third time.

Bill did not do anything unusual for the interval between then and what we now called "meat night." I was not certain what Ma did with the second piece of meat, but she made a beef stroganoff for the Sunday church supper that had everyone wanting her recipe.

I spent the remainder of the week teaching Bill how to run my paper route. The two bags were hung over the rear fender of my Flyer, which was okay, but when they were full, they dragged against the tire and made it hard to pedal. Bill had always run along with me when I did my route, so I tried placing the bags over his back and tying them under his stomach. I had to teach Bill not to jump, because the bags would slide off his back, but otherwise he accepted the additional burden. Bill did benefit, because several people on my route enjoyed the spectacle and gave him treats. I let him out each night as usual, and he returned on time without the mystery meat package.

Wednesday afternoon, Hack moved his bike over behind our garage so he would be ready to join the chase. I found a flashlight in the glove compartment of Pa's car and, though weak, the batteries still worked. We were ready. Ma had left supper out for me, and Bill and I shared it. Ma did not approve of my feeding him at the table, and Bill never begged when Ma was present.

Hack came over just before the news. The only change in Bill's routine came when I hooked him to a leash before going out so that we would not lose sight of him when we went to get the bikes. The night was clear with the moon almost full, so we had no trouble following Bill when I unhooked his leash. He ran at a slow trot, turning west instead of east at the school intersection. This was the main road to town and the river bridge.

The river divided the town in many ways; Pa once told me that the workers lived on the east side of the river and the owners resided on the west side up the hill, which was called Sugarloaf. It was a round hill which overlooked the downtown and factory district. The first settlers built on Sugarloaf because there was always a breeze and fewer mosquitoes.

None of us had seen much of that part of town except for one time when I subbed for a newspaper boy who delivered to part of Sugarloaf. Those routes were available to only a favored few as the Christmas gift money earned would keep us in groceries for a month. It soon became apparent that Bill was headed to Sugarloaf after we crossed the bridge.

The hill was steep and we pumped all the way up to keep in sight of Bill. I think he knew that we were following him, but he never looked back. Bill had a mission and a destination.

He led us to the left of the summit and turned down what I could remember was a dead end street. Bill went to the very end and without hesitation entered a driveway gate with two large "no trespassing" signs affixed to the posts. I knew it as the Mac-Nulty mansion. The MacNulty family had come to our town in the late 1800s to build a railroad out of the valley up to the coal mines. The mines had to use the MacNulty railroad to move coal from the mines down to be loaded on river barges. The MacNulty family made a fortune and it was rumored that none of the descendants had ever needed to work. The house was one of those old creepy Victorian brick affairs with a four-story tower in the front. Hack and I looked at each other for a moment and decided that "no trespassing" meant us, so we ditched our bikes and walked toward the rear of the house along the outside of the fence. We had lost Bill by this time because we could not see the front driveway from behind the fence.

I was about to give up when Hack yelled at me to get down. Headlights were visible now on the drive and they were headed our way. We watched from a prone position as a large truck passed us and stopped at the rear of the house. It then backed up to what looked like a basement door and two men got out of the cab. The door to the house opened, and two more men joined the truckers.

We soon knew the source of Bill's meat as the men used hand trucks to load white packages out of the house into the truck. They worked for what seemed like an eternity to us. As the last stack of meat was waiting to be loaded, we saw Bill, moving at an incredible speed, pick one of the packages off the hand truck and head down the drive. It looked like one of the men saw him for an instant as he turned to watch Bill make his exit. He swore, using a name for a female

dog, and then proceeded to finish loading the truck
with the other men. The truck backed up within inches
of where we were hiding and then disappeared down
the drive. The last sound that we heard was the clos-
ing of the gates that had been open when we arrived.
Bill had a good head start on us when we reached the
bikes, so we came off Sugarloaf Hill without ever
using our coaster brakes. When we got to my house,
Bill was on the porch waiting for us with his usual
weekly delivery. Hack headed home, and I put the
meat package in the refrigerator. When Ma got home
about a half hour later, Bill and I were in bed.

The next morning at breakfast, I told Ma that Bill
had come home with another package of meat, but she
had already looked in the refrigerator. I could tell that
Ma did not like what was going on because it did
seem that Bill was stealing meat from someone for our
table. Matters such as this were usually handled by Pa,
and Ma was having a hard time coming up with a
solution. I made a weak suggestion that we go to the
police, but she felt that, if anything was illegal, our
names would be all over page one of the town paper.

It was at this point that I decided to tell Ma exactly
what happened last night. I had never seen Ma turn
that pale white in the face before, and it was some
time before she said anything. She simply told me
that I had better get off to school before I was late for
class. I told Hack at recess that I had told Ma everything and he better not tell his mom anything or we
could be in real trouble. The whole adventure had me

so upset that I completely blew my history test after recess was over.

Ma and I had a long talk that evening. Bill sat by my feet, seeming to understand the serious nature of his escapades. Ma felt that what we had seen was some sort of a black market meat operation and, if we went to the police in person, those men could be after us once they knew our names. The police blotter was open to the paper and, to make matters worse, the chief and the newspaper publisher were brothers. Ma said that she would think about some solution and from now on Bill would be on a leash every Wednesday.

I had forgotten that Hack had given me a slip of paper when we'd parted company the night before. I pulled it out of my pocket. In true Hardy Boy fashion, Hack had noted the license number of the truck, probably when it had backed up to the fence before leaving. I did not know until later that Ma had waited till I was asleep to pen "stolen black market meat" and the license number on the last package.

She then rode my bike down to the police station and dropped the package of meat into the parking ticket return box by the front door.

Ma seemed quite composed at breakfast the next morning, and I thought that I should not discuss the meat matter any more. We talked briefly about my getting the billings out for my paper route before I headed off to school. Bill acted as if nothing had happened at all. After school I went down to the corner by

Main Street to pick up my papers to sort them for my route. I shared the packet with another carrier, so I always had to check the count. The headlines on page one almost made me faint dead away. It was all there, with headlines reading "Black Market Meat Ring Foiled," with most of the front page telling about the early morning raid at the MacNulty mansion. Several tons of meat had been found in a large basement cold storage locker, and three men were in jail. Two were MacNultys, and a third was a truck driver. I must have looked pretty grim, because when Jake, the other carrier, showed up, he asked me if I was all right. I muttered something and packed my papers in the bags for Bill. When I got home after my deliveries, I almost yelled at Ma about the headlines. She seemed pretty upset that someone in our town would steal meat from the war effort for sale in the black market. The paper went on to say that police had received an anonymous tip which led to the arrests.

It was about an hour after dinner that something hit me—my bike was not in the same place where I had left it last night. Somebody had ridden my bike after I had gone to bed, and only Ma and Hack knew about last night. I decided not to ask Ma about this before I had a chance to talk to Hack.

After dinner I made the excuse that Hack and I were going to study for the math test, and I left for his house. Hack was as surprised as I was with the feature in the paper. He swore that he had told no one. I related what I had found out about my bike, and I guess we both decided that Ma really had spilled the story to the police without telling them who she was.

I guess one of the worst moments of my life was the next day when I came home to see the chief's squad car parked in front of our house. Ma motioned Bill and me up on the porch, and the chief asked if Bill was my dog. I gave my best "yes sir." The next question was the tough one—where had I been at about 10:30 last Wednesday night? There was no way out of that one, so I told everything, including the fact that Hack had been with me. He asked that Ma and I go down to the station to have interviews taken. We picked up Hack on the way, leaving his mom speechless on their porch.

One of the men arrested had seen Bill and had described him to the police. The chief knew Bill was the dog because he had seen him many times with me on the paper route.

After we signed our statements, the chief led Ma, Hack, and me to his office. He introduced us to a very official looking man from the FBI, who actually congratulated us on the capture of the black market ringleaders. He passed out a citation to each of us, but it was not the citation that caused me to sit down. It was the government check for five hundred dollars that was attached to each citation. After the war Ma would get her new kitchen, and Hack and I had our first two years of college paid for.

It was a little hard to get used to being something of a hero in your hometown. Things got pretty much back to normal in about two weeks. I know Ma was proud of all of us and she wrote a long letter to Pa about winning our war on the home front. A month later, a very official package arrived addressed to Bill, in care of me. It contained the most beautiful engraved leather dog collar that I had ever seen. A plate was riveted to the leather with a serial number and the K-9 Corps designation. This was followed by a single silver star for valor. Bill was a K-9 hero.

Eventually the full story came out about the entire black market operation. The only men arrested in our town were the two MacNulty brothers. Rumor was that the rest of the family left town for their winter home in Florida. At any rate, a "For Sale" sign had replaced one of the gate "Keep Out" signs. Hack and I were told these things; we never went back to the place. Late in January, someone set fire to the mansion, and it burned to the ground in a spectacular fire. For a while the flames lit up the entire sky above Sugarloaf. People were pretty upset that all of this had happened in our town, and somebody probably wanted to make sure that no MacNulty ever returned. A picture in the paper taken after the fire showed only the foundation remaining, with the top of the meat cooler clearly visible.

7

No. 1 Scrappers

War kids grew up without parents. With our dads fighting and mothers doing all sorts of war work, we made our own way. I guess we missed our folks, but then there was also the freedom to do as we wished most of the time. Sometimes this freedom got us into trouble, sometimes it helped.

Every town must have had a haunted house and ours was no exception. We had a dandy—the old Peabody Sanitorium. Built in the 1880s by Dr. Peabody, the Victorian four-story brick structure reeked of ghosts. Stories of hangings and tortures added to the mystique of the place. It became our playground. I never knew who owned the sanitorium—it never occurred to us that the hollow shell with its rotting roof and broken windows belonged to anyone.

Inside, a stairway surrounded an iron-caged elevator shaft topped by a tower. Some of the rooms still had padding on the walls, and in one hall the floor was strewn with chains and ankle irons. That place at night tested your courage. I don't think I ever told Ma that we played in Peabody's Sanitorium.

So it was with some interest that I saw an article in our local paper one evening concerning the place. Our town now owned the building for back taxes and it was going to be demolished, with all the materials going to the war scrap drive. The mayor was asking for help from local contractors to do the work. We were about to lose our playground.

Scrap drives were pretty important to the war effort. Though future generations lost potential antique cars, old grillwork fences, and other artifacts, we won the war with that hidden resource. Scrap drives produced keen competition among us kids as we tried to compete for prizes for "most scrap," "best quality scrap," and other categories. The Boy Scouts were the crowd to beat—they were well organized and, we suspected, often received help in the form of donations from local factories. They had already stripped most of the iron fence and stair grill work from the sanitorium before we even thought of the place. Still, in the spirit of true competition, Hack thought another look was worth the effort.

Since the Scouts had the place overrun by day, we had to work at night. Hack loved to utter demonic screams and listen to their echo in the long, high-arched halls. It made my blood run cold.

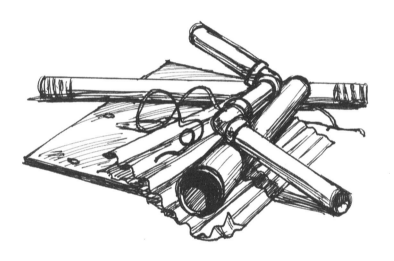

This night his yell was one of excitement. By prying open a panel behind one of the sinks, Hack had discovered that the sanitorium was plumbed with lead pipe. Lead was No. 1 on the scrap list.

To keep our discovery from the Scouts, we cut lengths of pipe with a saw and let them fall down the inside wall partitions to the basement. There we dragged the lengths out to our wagons. By day the Scouts came in and chopped away on the elevator cage.

We all worked pretty hard that week, and I got bawled out for falling asleep in school. We also lost a ball game to the west-side team. I could hardly swing the bat after sawing and lifting all that pipe. By week's end, we had almost all of the lead pipe out of the sanitorium and stacked in our garage. It was an impressive pile.

Saturday morning was scrap pickup day—the town truck would stop and weigh in any scrap you had. They were at our house over an hour hauling all that lead pipe out of our garage. That afternoon, Ma got a call for us to come down to the town hall.

We got the Grand Prize. The mayor gave us all a certificate and a $50 war bond.

They never got around to tearing down the Peabody place till after the war, and by then no one cared or wondered why almost all of the lead pipe was missing.

8

Know Thine
Enemy

Sitting on the hill, we watched old 75 coming up the grade into the draw. There was something alive about a steam locomotive, and the long flatcar loads of tanks and guns only added to the excitement. We could see the engineer with his red bandanna (he always waved) and knew the exact spot where he backed the quadrant into the company notch as No. 75 came over the hump and began the coast through the draw.

We were not there to watch trains, but to collect coal dropped alongside the tracks from the gondolas. Ma kept our furnace turned way down for the effort, and if I wanted a warm bedroom, I stoked the Armada in the upstairs hall. Hack and I would march up one side of the right-of-way till our feedbags were half full and then return on the opposite side. We never thought of it as work and nothing could replace that warm feeling coming from the Armada.

Ma always worried about the hobos—the drifters who rode the freight trains and often dropped off as the engine slowed on the grade. Now and then we would meet one of them—sometimes we'd talk briefly, but never got much from their alcohol-numbed brains. There was no romance to those hobos, only an earthly purgatory of sorts.

We watched two men jump off 75 and paid them little notice as we slid down into the draw. I kept an eye on them as they walked ahead of us—but as Hack was already collecting coal, I turned to my task and lost sight of the hobos as they disappeared into the woods. They were younger than most—probably draft dodgers, I thought.

A light snow was falling as we made our way back, bags now heavy with Illinois No. 16. Good coal it was—never made a clinker.

As we skirted the woods heading home, I smelled wood smoke. Hack was ahead of me, and I saw him stop short. When I reached him, I too saw the hobos sitting by a small fire staring at us through the veil of snow. The man nearest us got up and approached—he spoke to Hack in a slow, quiet voice with a strange accent. Hack motioned for me to sit down with the men. We'd never done that before, and I felt the lump in my throat growing.

Only one of the men talked—asking Hack directions and when the next train was due. Once I got up and put some additional wood on the fire, and the silent man smiled. Hobos never smiled. My initial fear began to be replaced by curiosity now; I was about to speak myself when Hack and the man suddenly rose and shook hands, and Hack motioned me to leave. As I left, the man who had remained silent grabbed my arm and thrust a small object into my hand. It was some sort of a coin.

I showed the coin to Hack on our way home—he couldn't make anything of it either except that the lettering was not American. By the time we got home the wind had picked up, driving the snow into our faces. My thoughts left the hobos and turned to firing up the Armada. Ma made me take a bath after collecting coal. I hung my towel and clean clothes on a chair beside the glowing stove. A hot tub and warm clothes were real luxury.

I usually helped Hack with his paper route so he'd have more time to play. We always picked up yesterday's paper for the paper drive at the same time. It was a good two-man job.

I think Hack saw the headline banner first as we folded the papers. Two escaped German POWs had been captured south of town and returned to a camp about fifty miles to the south. I could feel the cold sweat forming on my back. Hack looked downright pale.

Later, at home, I pulled the strange coin from my pants pocket. It looked sinister now, almost evil. I held it in my fist for what seemed like hours, and then I opened the door of the Armada and tossed it among the glowing coals.

9

Charlie's Garwood and the One That Got Away

When we weren't throwing the baseball, we were fishing. Fishing was free, and we even caught something worth keeping once in a while. Ma always ditched any carp in the victory garden.

We had to bike about seven miles to Simpson's Lake, but you could always cool off with a swim when you got there. The water was clear and cool, even in midsummer—not like the creek that ran behind our house. Green slime and bullfrogs were about all that creek had to offer.

Simpson's Lake was named after the Simpson family—all I knew about them now was that they had money. They seemed to buy everything new every year; this year it was Charlie's Garwood. Charlie Simp-

son was just plain dumb, so it was good for him that he
was rich. Charlie was older than we were and should
have been out of school. I often thought that he kept
flunking so he wouldn't get drafted. Charlie also loved
to show off, and that made all of us hate him.

Well, this summer Charlie's dad had bought him
a Garwood inboard boat. That thing was beautiful,
all chrome and varnished mahogany. It planed eas-
ily, and the massive eight-cylinder engine roared like
distant thunder. We could tell when Charlie was
drunk; he'd sit out in the middle of Simpson's Lake
and just gun that big engine. About that time, we
would quit fishing.

I guess that this summer would have been much the
same, with our watching Charlie roar around the lake,
except that Andy's dad who ran the Civil Defense
Corps gave us some old gas masks. By the time I saw
them, Andy and Hack had converted the masks to
swim snorkels by attaching a piece of milking machine
hose and balsa wood float to the canister tube. Swim-
ming took on a new dimension. After a trial in my bath-
tub, which was brief because Ma kicked us out when
water droplets formed on the kitchen ceiling, we
headed to Simpson's Lake for the big water.

We spent hours that day drifting along beneath
the surface, watching the fish and painted turtles
among the eel grass. We stopped only when lunch
time was signaled by our growling stomachs.

Charlie did his best to ruin our afternoon—the
Garwood was full of his drinking buddies, and he

came so close to the shore that we were afraid to swim at all. By late afternoon they had settled down to fishing and discharging beer cans into the water. Hack sought revenge.

Charlie and his friends were far too drunk to see three small floats and hoses approaching the Garwood. Hack's plan was sheer genius; carefully, we tied all of the fishing lines together under the Garwood. Andy and I made for shore. Hack gave one giant pull on the lines and followed.

Pandemonium had broken loose in Charlie's Garwood by the time I made the beach. All those drunks were trying to pull in their lines, and the more they pulled, the more convinced they were that they had all caught the big one. I was so weak from laughter that I hardly noticed people falling out of the boat into the water.

Anyway, for some reason, Charlie in his stupor decided to head for home and put the Garwood in gear. Later we found out that Charlie put that boat right through his dock and the Garwood, with Charlie still in it, ended up in the middle of the front yard. You could hear Charlie's old man all the way across the lake.

Well, the rest of the summer went pretty quiet out at Simpson's Lake without Charlie. The only real noise came out of Angelica when Andy convinced her to try one of our snorkels and a crawdad bit her.

10

The Flume

Spring always brought high water to the creek, and high water signaled that it was time for the county canoe race. The banks put up war bonds for prizes, something that guaranteed fierce competition. We also had a healthy dislike for the Grantsville school kids with their fancy canoes and brand new paddles. Our town couldn't afford to outfit us, so we borrowed our equipment from whoever was willing to take the risk. More than one canoe ended up on a submerged stump, holed.

We always drew lots for teams—it was only fair. I'd never been in the winners' circle, but Andy came in third in last year's race. I was hoping to get paired off with him. No such luck; when I called my number,

Angelica stepped forward. It was tough, I really liked Angelica, but my chances of placing ended right there. When she walked over, I forced a smile and gave her a slap on the back. Angelica understood.

One thing was in our favor—Angelica's dad let us use his new seventeen-foot Old Town. Most of us got out before the race to practice on the Mill Pond. I let Angelica stern so I could put some speed into the bow stroke. It was nice out on the pond, and I think Angelica was really trying. By afternoon's end she had a pretty good "J."

The race always began at Crystal Bridge with a good five-mile run to the pond. You had to portage around the dam and old Nelson Mill, and run another two miles or so to the town park. The portage was bad; if you weren't one of the first in line for the take-out, you'd had it.

The Nelson Mill, built in the 1850s, was silent now. The big undershot wheel was gone and water leaked from the half-rotten wood flume. The water discharged through a stone tunnel under the mill and returned to the creek. We'd pulled our canoe out of the flume gate and Angelica was tossing milkweed pods into the flume while we waited for her dad to pick us up. Suddenly she looked me in the eye and asked why we couldn't run the flume and tunnel with the canoe to avoid the portage. First I told her she was crazy, and then I found myself pushing the canoe back into the water above the flume gate, waiting for Angelica to run down to the outlet. When I saw her, I

let the empty canoe drift into the flume. I watched with horror as the craft picked up speed and disappeared into the tunnel. It seemed like hours. But seconds later Angelica retrieved the canoe intact and paddled across the creek to the park. No one observed her, or our trial.

The start at Crystal was plain excitement. Canoes jammed the creek from bank to bank when Doc Hawkins started us with his cannon. We were at least up in the front pack, and I could hear yells behind us as several canoes overturned in the first rill. Soon, I saw the Mill Pond coming into view, and the realization that we were going down that flume gave me the chills. Already, the four lead canoes were lined up at the portage path. We eased over to the other side of the creek and entered the raceway.

I don't recall much about the next few minutes except that we both lay down flat in the bottom, and all around us was the roar of water and darkness. Then I opened my eyes to sunlight and bulrushes— we'd made it!

I never knew that I could paddle so fast, but for the last lap we were both so inspired by being out in front that I don't think anyone could have caught up with us. Doc's cannon boomed again—we'd won.

There were a few scratches on Angelica's dad's canoe, but he didn't seem to mind. Grantsville protested too, but Doc backed us up. Next year the flume would be illegal, but we'd won fair and square.

I ate supper with Angelica's family that evening—we were all pretty excited; but excitement gave way to fatigue as we sat together on the porch swing. The smell of lilacs filled the warm evening air. Neither of us said anything for a long time, then Angelica held my face for a moment and kissed me quickly. The war was forgotten for a time—Angelica was soon asleep, her head on my shoulder. Later I got up quietly so as not to disturb her and walked slowly home with my prize war bond in my hand. It was dawn now in Normandy as the first wave hit Omaha Beach.

11

The Snake Pit

Old man Anderson hated snakes—he disliked most anything that lived, but snakes were at the top of his list. Before the war, Anderson had a hired man who worked in his yard. That man didn't seem to mind snakes, but old man Anderson would hardly cut grass for fear of seeing one of those critters.

Most of our homes still had cisterns, and when our foundry got the tank turret contract, we were told to use town water for drinking only. I guess they needed a lot of water or something to cool the iron. Anyway, when old man Anderson opened his cistern pit to reconnect the line, it was crawling with snakes. That cool brickwork was snake heaven.

Anderson wouldn't talk to us, but he told Ma that if we would clean out that pit we'd get a nickel for every one we caught. I got Pa's kerosene fishing lantern working, Andy borrowed a ladder from his dad's shop, and Hack knew someone in the town hall who had a bar to raise the cast-iron lid off the pit. We were in the snake removal business.

God, that pit was dark, even with the lantern. We took turns climbing down the ladder and pulling snakes out of the brickwork. We'd heave them out, and whoever was up top put them in a bushel basket. They didn't move much in the cool spring weather, so that basket took on the look of snake spaghetti. We kept a count. Old man Anderson took our word for the sum of two hundred plus reptiles, and that ten-dollar bill was a small fortune to us.

None of us had thought of disposing of two hundred snakes—wherever we dumped them, it would hardly go unnoticed. Besides, the snakes were now so intertwined in that wood basket that we would never get them out. I hadn't noticed, but we were walking across the corner of Mrs. Wilson's garden; Mrs. Wilson did notice and for several moments vented her verbal wrath on us. The Lord took a real beating before she slammed the door with threats to call the police or something. She also, without knowing it, solved our snake-disposal problem.

Mrs. Wilson always left her basement laundry room window ajar, and late that evening a bushel basket was carefully lowered through that window to her basement floor.

Mrs. Wilson was part English, or at least she liked to think she was. I know she always had afternoon tea and invited in a bunch of old ladies who had nothing more to do than talk about other people.

Meanwhile, through the night, those snakes had warmed up and were enjoying the warmth of the salamander furnace pipes. The first hint of trouble came when the furnace blower came on and one of our more substantial specimens dropped out of the ceiling vent and landed on the neck of Mrs. Wilson's bridge partner.

From what we heard later, snakes were popping out of every hot-air register in that house. The unfortunate matron with the reptile necklace was the first to exit through the porch screen door without pausing to open it. Within seconds, Mrs. Wilson was alone with some broken china and all those snakes. I don't know if Mrs. Wilson paid those firemen a nickel for each snake they found or not, but she spent a week with her sister over in Grantsville.

12

Jimmey

There was not much question that I needed eyeglasses. Ma had caught me again with my nose almost touching my homework, and my writing was also getting pretty hard to read. I didn't like the idea of wearing glasses. They looked weird to start with and fell off your face when you were playing any sport. But Ma was right, and glasses meant a visit to Doctor Osida.

His office was downtown in a small building next to the dime store. A large eye was painted on the front plate-glass window with his name below. I didn't know much about Doctor Osida or his family other than he had two kids. Jimmey was in my grade at school, and his sister Sue was older by at least one grade. At one time Ma had asked me to see if Jimmey would help me with my math because it was one subject I could not understand at all. My math grades were barely passing. Part of my problem might be my eyesight, I thought, because I did have trouble seeing the numbers on the blackboard.

Ma took me down later that week to visit Doctor Osida's office. The interior was filled with cases containing what seemed like hundreds of pairs of glasses, and the walls were covered with framed documents written in some Oriental language. Ma thought that the Osida family had come from San Francisco during the Depression. Doctor Osida's English was a little strange, but Jimmey sounded like all the rest of us.

The doctor placed me in a high chair facing a number of rolled up scrolls on the back wall of his office. I spent about a half hour looking at letters and numbers, with the result being a pair of metal frames which made me look like a walking microscope. But I had to admit that I could see a lot better. As we were leaving the store, Jimmey was returning from school and Ma bugged me to ask him for help with my math. Jimmey worked afternoons cleaning the glasses cases. I would meet him tomorrow at the store for my first lesson. Between new glasses and help from Jimmey, I might get a passing grade this year.

The next day I was the brunt of a few jokes aimed at my new frames. Angelica said I looked like a little old professor; most of the other comments were less kind. I did find that at recess I never missed catching a fielded ball.

After school, I met Jimmey, and we walked down to his dad's store. He suggested that we go upstairs so that we would not disturb his dad's customers. The upstairs was filled with all kinds of strange machines that Jimmey said were used to grind eyeglass lenses. A rear room had a long table with a telescope-like affair on the top. This was an optical bench, according to Jimmey.

We pulled two chairs away from the tables and set to work on my next math lesson. It did not take me long to realize that Jimmey was a math brain. He could just look at a math word problem and give me the answer. He was a good teacher and explained each step much better than old Mr. Elsemann, who was our math teacher. We must have spent two hours on my studies, and when I left the store I was thinking that Jimmey was okay.

The next day at recess I introduced Jimmey to our gang. Our talk turned to baseball, as we had a game that afternoon. Jimmey said that he had played a little baseball at another school and would like to watch our game.

Our next game was with Windsor on our field. They were a new school in our league. We had not had a good season that year, because our best pitcher had moved with his family to another town, and our catcher had broken his wrist on a bad catch. We were the smallest school in the league, so replacements were hard to find. I did not pick the best game for Jimmey to watch; Windsor shut us out 9–0. We managed to get only three runners on base and two of those were taken out on a double play. Coach was pretty upset with our showing and didn't even come back to the locker room after the game. Our next practice was going to be a long one.

Jimmey and I had been at my math homework for about two hours when he changed the subject from math to baseball. We had another game coming up the end of the week, and I did not look forward to a repeat of Windsor. When Jimmey started talking about that game, I saw that he knew a lot more about baseball than I had thought. In fact he talked a better game than our coach. I invited him to our next practice.

It was not a good introduction. As expected, our coach was in a foul mood and spent half the time telling us how dumb we were. We did get a little time to play, and Jimmey asked me if he could try to pitch a few balls. Our pitcher was having a hard time just getting the ball over the plate, so coach gave Jimmey some time on the mound.

The first thing I saw was his windup, which looked as if he was going to come off the mound. His first ball came in so fast that our catcher didn't even see it go by his mitt. Jimmey pitched about ten strike balls in a row, and none of our hitters came close to connecting with a ball. Coach sat there with his jaw in his lap. When Jimmey walked off the mound, we all cheered him. He had brought us back together.

Our next game was an away event with Rockland. They were a tough bunch and had three heavy hitters who could be counted on for runs whenever they came to bat. This was going to be a real test for our new pitcher. When Jimmey walked out to the mound for the first time, I heard a few boos from the crowd. I didn't think much of it, but things would not get any better. I guess I had never seen anything like how he could pitch. We actually won 2–1, with Jimmey letting only one hit go by.

The crowd got real ugly at the end, calling us a bunch of dirty Japs, among other insults. We surrounded Jimmey and walked off the field directly to our bus. Two of their players followed us and even threw a couple of rocks at the bus as we left. It was my first experience with this kind of thing, and my first reaction was to return and fight. Coach told us to concentrate on the fact that we as a team won the game, and no amount of insults could take that away from us. He appointed Jimmey as our pitcher and added that he didn't give a damn who we were or where we came from. I thought it was one of coach's better pep talks.

That was the worst crowd we had to endure all season, but there were always some individuals at each game who yelled insults at Jimmey. As far as I could tell, they went by him. We never talked about these things during my math sessions, and as far as I could tell Jimmey and his family were just as good Americans as the rest of us.

Ma and I had some long talks about Jimmey and all of the insults he got at our games. Our team had two players with German names and one Italian, and these members of our team never got any flack from the bleachers. Ma said that prejudice didn't make any sense, so I should not try to justify it on any basis. Jimmey was my friend and his family were all good citizens of our town.

Things sort of tapered off after baseball season, and Jimmey and I concentrated on my math. Thanks to Jimmey, I had a "B" in that course by Christmas, a fact Ma considered a minor miracle. I was also able to watch Jimmey's father work in his shop grinding glass lenses for his business. Customers seldom had to wait for glasses because Doctor Osida had an endless inventory and could accommodate almost any eye correction need. He had made a telescope for Jimmey, which we took up to the park on top of Sugarloaf Hill several evenings to watch the stars. Jimmey knew many of the planet formations and would aim the telescope, telling me each time what I was about to see. Jimmey was sort of a scientist, to my way of thinking.

After Christmas, I saw very little of Ma because her factory had been awarded a contract to make a new bombsight called a Norton. It was a very complicated device, but the enemy had nothing like it for accurate bombing. Ma was in charge of the final assembly, and she was investigated by the FBI to make sure that she was a good American. She had a special name tag which had to be worn to get into her part of the factory. She also stopped talking about the specifics of her job. There were times that I ate cereal three times a day.

My grades improved because most of my friends were also too busy doing without parents. Ma would leave me a list every day telling me what needed to be done while she was at work. I began to see that something was not going well at the plant, because Ma was becoming irritable during the brief times I was with her. I thought that the new bombsight was not going together as planned. Jimmey's family was having a bad time, too. Business was off and someone had tossed a brick through the painted "eye" on his plate-glass store window.

I happened to have the news on the radio after listening to Captain Midnight one night, and the commentator was talking about President Roosevelt announcing that Japanese Americans were going to be sent to some kind of a prison camp. It made no sense to me, so the next day I asked Jimmey about the announcement. I could see that he was not his usual self, and he just nodded his head when I asked if he had to move. My first thought was a selfish one: we would lose our star pitcher. Later, I started thinking of his family losing their home and store.

I waited up late until Ma came home that night so I could ask her about President Roosevelt's announcement. She explained that our government had the notion that Japanese people in America could possibly become spies and feed information back to Japan. It was hard to believe that Doctor Osida was a spy.

We needed him because there was no one else to make glasses for our town. Ma was really mad about the whole thing; she seldom commented on matters of government, but she almost seemed ready to fight for the Osida family.

Ma had been employed for almost the entire duration of the war. I could hardly remember when we would all sit together for an evening meal. Ma had changed and seemed a lot tougher in ways. I also felt that I was no longer a little boy, and the war more than age had affected me. Ma started out in the typical Rosie the Riveter jobs, but now she was managing a staff of workers trying to assemble the bombsight. Things had only gotten worse, and now a team of so-called military experts had appeared at the plant and were looking over everyone's shoulder. The leader was a full bird who suspected every worker of sabotage.

Angelica had come over to have a "sandwich" dinner with us because she and I were co-chairs for the spring dance. When Ma arrived home, the conversation turned to the bombsight. I guess it was Angelica who suggested the solution: call in Doctor Osida. I almost laughed at that idea, because that bird colonel would probably throw the doctor in prison as soon as he saw that Osida was Japanese. I did agree that the doctor was smart enough to give some help, but there was no way to involve him with all those military types wandering around the factory.

Our discussion turned back to the dance arrangements, which were limited because there were no

bands for music. The school had a record player and
public address system, so we decided to ask our
classmates to bring their favorite records. A lot of our
recordings were pretty old because no new records
were being made except for war promotions. That
music was mostly marches, and "missing you"
songs. We would also draw for a fifty-dollar war
bond, which we would pay for with money from
ticket sales.

I walked Angelica home and spent some time
with her on her porch swing. There just seemed to be
so little private time anymore for us to enjoy. We
kissed a lot that night; it was as if we were afraid
something was going to happen to take us away from
each other.

Ma was late as usual getting home the next day,
which generally meant cold cuts or grilled Spam
sandwiches. I can't remember ever being hungry
since only the same old food was on the table each
night. After I had finished with the dishes, Ma sat
down with me and said that she had a secret to share.
She opened her lunch pail, and instead of the usual
paper bag, she pulled out one of the bombsight lens
assemblies. I was so scared that I wanted to run out of
the house. While I was thinking about how many
years I would be spending in jail, Ma explained that
she wanted me to take the lens to Doctor Osida
tomorrow. She could cover up the loss for a day, but
no more. Well, I thought, at least we might be able to
share a jail cell together.

At school I confided with Jimmey and agreed to meet at his father's office after school. Jimmey felt that it would be hard to do much in one day, but he felt that the doctor would want to try. We would need some help in making something called shims, which required careful cutting of paper, so I recruited Angelica. She acted like she enjoyed the sport of putting one over on the colonel and his team. After school, I went home and used a paper bag to carry the sight lens to the office. Angelica met me there, and Doctor Osida showed us upstairs to his workshop.

Doctor Osida's English was not all that good, so Jimmey helped to translate his instructions to us. First he dismantled the lens assembly and placed all of the individual lenses on his optical bench. Then he moved each lens to get some kind of an alignment. Angelica was told to cut a number of paper shims using a protractor and razor blade. The Doctor explained that these shims would be used as spacers to maintain the proper distance between each lens once that measurement was known.

Next he turned and took me over to several machines Jimmey translated as laps. Doctor Osida fastened the lens to the lower plate using beeswax, and the upper plate was some type of grinding stone that rotated very fast. I had to stand by each lap and time the grinding operation. I would then shut the machine off and Doctor Osida would inspect my work. The final grinding was done with some type of fine powder to polish any scratches out of the lens.

Jimmey told me that this is how his father made all of his glasses for his store.

I lost track of time, but Jimmey's mother had called our mas and told them not to worry. She made up some very strong tea, which was also sweet, and I am sure that this brew helped us stay awake. Doctor Osida did the final re-assembly of the lenses and made a final check on the optical bench. He said nothing, but smiled at us and shook our hands. I knew that we had a winner.

Angelica and I walked home together, and by the time I walked into the kitchen Ma was cooking her breakfast. I gave her the lens and saw that it was six a.m. in the morning.

I remembered little from school that day. I watched Angelica doze off in study hall, and I slept through recess and lunch. Somehow, I made it home that afternoon and, had it not been for Bill, I would not have completed my paper route. When Ma came home, she found me fast asleep on my bed. She did not wake me but fed and walked Bill herself.

When I awoke the next morning, I still had all of my clothes on, and it took me a few minutes to figure out that I was home. I cleaned myself up as best I could and ran downstairs to ask Ma how the rebuilt bombsight lens had worked out. She was brief, only saying everything was okay, and that I should thank Doctor Osida for his help. I was about to press her for more details when I noticed that she was completely wrung out herself. I figured I'd best drop the subject and head for school.

When I reached the playground, Angelica gave me a big hug and asked if I had heard what a hero my Ma was. When Angelica finished her story, I knew why Ma looked so beat this morning. She had taken the lens assembly to work and had it assembled into a complete unit. She then placed it on the final inspection table for the bird colonel and his team to test. Ma was the only one who knew the sight was special. After the inspection, the colonel announced that not only had the optical problem been corrected, but this bombsight far exceeded the performance specifications. When the plant manager asked Ma how she had corrected the problem, she explained that it was due to the genius of Doctor Osida, and he was the only one who could reproduce the work. At the name Osida, the bird about blew up, from what Angelica heard. When he started in about Japs, and that all Japanese were spies, Ma held her ground and told that bird that without Doctor Osida there would be no bombsights. Angelica said she heard Ma was so mad that she was shaking all over.

I guess that the colonel had met his match in Ma, because he turned and walked to the plant office where he disappeared for a half hour. Everyone knew that the telephone line to Washington D.C. was red hot. When the colonel returned to the inspection table, he looked like he'd been defeated in battle. He simply said to Ma that Doctor Osida and his family would stay in our town, and that the doctor would be in charge of the lens production. As the colonel turned to leave, a few of Ma's workers started clapping. The clap turned into a roar, and Ma was hoisted on the shoulders of two of her workers for a grand parade around the plant floor.

There was a rumor that Ma was given a reward of one week's pay by the plant manager. I was so hopped up after hearing Angelica's story that I missed another day of knowing what most of my teachers said to me. I did notice that many of my friends were gathering around Jimmey and slapping him on the back. When I got home that afternoon, there was a crowd waiting to welcome Ma. When she arrived, there were more cheers from her workers. A small lady (Mrs. Osida) pushed her way up to Ma, bowed, and presented her with a vase full of hand-made paper flowers. People hugged, slapped each other on the back, and cheered some more. I went to the back porch inside to rescue Bill, who was hiding under the kitchen table.

There were two other incidents that were related to the bombsight incident. First, Jimmey never received another boo during a baseball game. He was just another American, which made the rest of us feel pretty good. We won the next conference, and I think that it was Jimmey who brought us together.

Second, the next weekend after Doctor Osida had saved the bombsight program, a team of men showed up at his store. By the end of the day, the place had a new coat of paint inside and out along with a new front plate-glass window. Angelica's mother had painted a new "eye" just like the old one. There was one addition, however; a pole was placed beside the entrance with an American flag flying proudly. I always felt that in addition to Ma, Doctor Osida was a person of courage. He certainly had to know that the precision bombsight would be used against Japan.

13

Homecoming

I heard old Snake Eyes on the school page during lunch hollering for Angelica. Snake Eyes never talked. He hollered at everyone. Maybe that was why he was school principal. I had returned to chewing my way through a day-old sandwich when I caught sight of Angelica, on the run, cutting across the ball field. She was also yelling at the top of her lungs. Hack looked at me like I should know what was going on. I shook my head as the bell rang.

Word got around pretty fast during the afternoon about Angelica, though. The Allies had liberated a German POW camp and Marco, her brother who had been missing in action, was coming home. He was also some kind of a hero. My mind went blank as far as school was concerned for the rest of the afternoon.

I think every member of the ball team headed for Angelica's after school. We were supposed to have a ball game—I guess it never came off 'cause none of us showed. There was a big crowd around Angelica's house when we got there, and for a while I wondered if we'd see her. Angelica's eyes were red and swollen—she would start talking to us and all of a sudden the tears would come.

Marco had been shot down on a bombing run over Germany. He crash-landed the plane and, though he had been shot in the arm and had lost a leg below the knee, he managed to pull his six crewmen from the flaming wreckage before passing out from loss of blood. Marco was coming home with a battle commission and the Medal of Honor. No one in our town had ever been given that honor. It was the turning point in the war for all of us—we knew that we were going to win.

I'd never seen people so friendly—even Anderson smiled at us—once. The town was cleaned from one end to the other for Marco's homecoming, with trimmed lawns, polished cars, and flowers everywhere. Some men showed up one evening and completely repainted Angelica's folks' house too. I wished our town could be like that all the time. Even the Graverly started on the first crank.

It was one of those perfect summer days with a blue midwestern sky and bright sun making everything technicolor. The crowd at the station started to cheer as the plume from the Southwest Limited came

into view. The engineer had her banked and the cocks closed as 4983 slowed to a stop. Then everything started to happen at once. The crowd went wild as the band struck up and firecrackers popped everywhere. Then there was a strange instant silence as a mother and her son were reunited. I caught a brief glimpse of Marco with Angelica as they stepped into Mr. Kingsley's Lincoln convertible. Half the people in town were part of the parade that followed to the town square.

Marco's family was up on a stage erected in front of the war memorial. You could hardly see them with all the flags and flowers. Someone told us that Mrs. Wilson had picked her entire garden for the occasion.

Marco was stiff at attention—one hand on his crutch. Slowly, the general rose, and even under all that brass he seemed almost a part of Marco's family with a sincere kind smile and a hug for Marco's mom. I couldn't take my eyes off Angelica with her white dress and auburn hair moving in rhythm with the light breeze. I caught myself thinking how beautiful she was. She saw me for a moment and, in that moment, I think she knew everything I was thinking.

The general was brief in his remarks, and when he presented the Medal of Honor to Marco with his mother at his side, all I could hear was people blowing their noses. The band closed with the national anthem and a moment of silence for those yet across. I noticed that the general also used his handkerchief.

Ma and I waited till after supper to pay our respects—by then I think Marco had shaken the hand of everyone in our town. I'd about run out of nice things to say when Angelica rescued me to take a walk. She'd talk for a spell and then fall silent. Marco would work with her dad now—the war was over for him, and maybe it would end before Angelica's other brother would have to go. I had another year of school and then...

We paused by the pond, and for a moment Angelica was silhouetted against the moon beside me. I started saying all sorts of strange things to her, trying to get my feelings out. Gently, she placed her finger across my lips. We must have kissed each other for what seemed like an eternity. After that we started home, stopping frequently to hold each other very close. When we got back to Angelica's house Ma saw us, and by her look I knew she also understood everything.

14

Star of the Show

Carnies or carnivals provided one of the few pleasant distractions from the war effort for us. Rides, bright lights, the smell of popcorn, and sideshows that by today's standards would be x-rated entertainment. I don't remember my folks ever attending a previous carnival, but I was always allowed one night in that wild and wicked world.

They'd set up early in the morning on the edge of town. There were always jobs to be had, so we would line up for roustabout with the sun on the horizon. This year, May's shows had an added attraction—an air stunt show. Hack and I moved over to the line in front of those two gleaming Stinson biplanes. We must have looked eager, 'cause an old man looking more like a shaggy dog than anything human gave us some rags and polish and escorted us to the planes. Polishing airplanes is a hard way to earn a free pass, but somehow all of the mystique of the brave fighter pilots ducking the enemy was caught up in those Stinsons.

About noon we saw our first real, live pilot. And he looked like the war posters with the leather jacket, helmet, and goggles. We received little more than a glance as he busied himself with inspecting the airframe and engine. I'd never seen so many cables and wires, but he acted like he knew what they were all used for. I caught a glance of Hack, in his usual fashion, asking questions of the pilot.

Carnival food was good—simple, and plentiful. We sat across from our pilot and after a fashion he befriended us. One plane was kept as a backup and they also had a third one for spare parts. Some of the stunt routines made my stomach turn at the mention. I downed the meatloaf with a final glass of lemonade and we headed back to an afternoon of polishing under the hot sun. Hack was spending a lot of time with the pilot now.

They must have liked our work, 'cause we got our passes plus a dozen ride tickets and a dollar tip each from the pilot. As we rode home on our bikes, Hank told me he would be late getting to the stands for the air show. Something was up, but he offered no explanation.

For the first time, my mom said she'd go with me to the carnival air show. Maybe it was because I was taking Angelica and Mom knew I wouldn't go into any of the peep shows on the strip. It was one of those hot, humid summer nights with haze over the horizon—even the flies sounded like they were fighting the thick air. We filled ourselves with cotton candy and used up all the ride tickets. I was ready to sit down when they announced the air show over the P.A.

We watched the biplane take off in the field. I thought of all that dust on our wax polish as the plane rose almost straight up and did a series of rolls. Red smoke trailed from wingtip flares. My mind drifted for a moment to those fliers in the war who were dodging bullets instead of pleasing crowds. I think my mom's mind was on the same track.

For the final run, the pilot put the plane into a steep dive, pulling out for a run upside down just above the stand. As he roared by amid the screams of the spectators, I discovered why Hack had not joined us. He was in the rear cockpit, hanging upside down in the safety harness. Unfortunately for Hack, my mom also saw his pale, white face as the pilot zoomed off in a trail of acrid red smoke.

Hack was grounded for a week after that event, and all I could do was to wave at him as I passed on my paper route. Later he told me that he lost his lunch on the first roll but that things went pretty well after that. We kept the firecrackers he was supposed to light off as he passed the stand for Fourth of July. I think sheer terror prevented Hack from doing anything but hanging on for his life.

15

Halloween and the Last of the Real Live Ghosts

I guess we never got into any real bad trouble, but Flash (our name for our local police chief) kept track of us. We had sort of an honorable truce, but once every year it was broken—on Halloween night. Halloween was well placed on the calendar—between Fourth of July and Christmas. Our firecracker scars had pretty well healed, and anything we did that was bad was forgotten by Christmas.

Probably because of last year's garbage can spectacular, where we lined the street with over a hundred cans tied handle to handle and pulled them over like dominoes, Flash and the town fathers decided to have a school Halloween party.

I had mixed emotions about it—Angelica had invited me to the party and costume dance, but to miss our usual night of tricks was another matter. Andy was the first to suggest that the party needed an uninvited guest—a ghost.

Hack and Andy made up the best ghost I'd ever seen, with some costume help from Angelica. The head was a papier-mâché skull with glowing red flashlight bulbs for eyes, and Angelica had made a long, flowing cape from sheeting. I made "bone" hands from oak twigs and wire, and the body consisted of several real rubber balloons saved from pre-war days. We left it in Andy's dad's office at the shop so that he could get the full effect of the apparition hanging from the ceiling.

But the next afternoon, Andy's dad had a surprise for us. He had filled the balloons with just enough hydrogen from the welder tank. By properly weighting our ghost, you could make it look like it was floating just off the ground. Andy's dad was perfect that way—he knew just when to help us, and when to step aside.

Our plan on Halloween night was to attach our ghost to a long run of kite string and, at dance intermission time, pull it along the sidewalk to the gym entrance. Hopefully there would be enough kids outside for a good effect.

Flash had only one real adversary that I knew of—Silas Henry. Old Silas lived in a shack on the far side of the Mill Pond and made moonshine. I think he

lived on the stuff, because his brain and eyesight were half gone. Silas was mean, too, so we kept our distance. Flash took an instant dislike to Silas and would run him out of town almost every time they met, which was usually in front of Rollf's Tavern. It was rumored that Silas kept a stash of gold coins buried near his shack, but we never dared go near the place. For some strange reason, Silas decided to come into town on Halloween night.

The party really was nice, and I spent most of my time dancing with Angelica. She came dressed in a gypsy costume, filling it out in a way that almost made me forget our intermission stunt. It was warm for Halloween, and we had a good crowd in front of the gym when Hack took the slack out of the kite string, Andy switched on the red "eyes," and I let the ghost go free from behind a tree.

Maybe old Silas was attracted by the screams as our ghost took full effect, or maybe he saw Flash headed our way with his nose hot on the scent of trouble. We'll never know, because about the time Flash made an attempt to grab Silas, Silas saw our ghost. Probably for a fleeting moment, Silas's mind went dead sober, but it was for certain that Silas collided with our ghost in blind fright at the gym entrance.

Our Halloween work of art, now covering most of Silas, picked up considerable speed as he raced through the gym and out the girl's locker room exit. Flash was right after him, and I got to admit that he stayed with Silas up to the end of Mill Road where

Silas ducked into the briars. Flash, not being crazed with fear and booze, rested his case at that point. They said later than Silas's trail through the briars was marked by shreds of torn sheet.

The Halloween party was a real success, even without a live ghost, and the ticket money added two hundred dollars to our school bond drive. I'll never forget that ghost, but I'll also never forget how nice Angelica looked and how I didn't want to stop kissing her goodnight.

16

The Gift

Christmas was one of the few times we forgot about the war effort and relaxed a bit from our world of coupons and controls. We rationed out our own meat coupons so that a real beef roast would grace our table on Christmas Day. And then there was always a Christmas letter from Pa under the tree. Ma always saved it to read on Christmas Day.

But this Christmas started in the fall for us. Angelica's mom had contacted a relative living in a small, war-torn village in France. The idea was for our church to share Christmas in some way with theirs, and we had to have everything ready by mid-October. It was Angelica who suggested that we collect and repair some old toys.

Andy's dad's shop took on the look of Santa's workshop as we turned the back room into our repair center. Angelica and two of her friends worked on the dolls, and we stayed with the mechanical and painting tasks. I guess the Christmas spirit caught on early, because one day old man Anderson yelled at us as we were passing by and gave us an old doll house that had belonged to his mother. By the time we had it rebuilt, it was a real treasure, complete with fresh paint, furniture, and lace curtains in the windows.

We made our date with all the toys carefully boxed in a large wood crate and loaded on Andy's dad's pickup truck late Sunday. Also inside was a large greeting card containing all of our names and a Christmas greeting in French. Angelica's mother had taught French in the old country and she said some nice things for us. Old 75 steamed away from the station that Monday morning with our cargo.

We sort of forgot about that village far off in France with all the excitement of our own holiday season. We always shared Christmas Eve with Angelica's family, which was fine with me. Anyway, as I sat beside Angelica that special night in church, I sensed something special. So I was not too surprised to see her mother walk to the front of the church just before the end of the service. She was carrying a flat package that looked something like a book. She first translated a Christmas greeting for all of us from our French village. That message left all of us pretty quiet, and then she opened the package. It was a phono-

graph record. Someone pushed the old church phono-
graph up in front of the altar, and for a spell our
church filled with the sound of French children's
voices singing their thanks to us in traditional French
Christmas carols. There wasn't a dry eye in the place
after the benediction.

We heard later that an American flier shot down
near that town had been rescued by some of the
French villagers and had carried the record back to
the U.S. When the airman's senior officer was told the
story of our Christmas "exchange," he had a special
courier deliver the package to Angelica's home.

That Christmas night, as Angelica and I stepped
out into the cold night with our families, the joyful
spirit of a small French village was with all of us. We
had given so little, and had received so much in return.

17

Celebration

I guess the war might have gone on forever as far as we kids were concerned. Most of us had grown up without fathers, and war work also consumed much of our mothers' time too. So it was hard to imagine that the war would end, but end it would. Graduation, though, came first.

For us, graduation was always an evening event. Nights were cooler, and at least the day shift could attend. Still, as we filed quietly in, row by row, the night air was heavy, and a rumble now and then told of a coming storm. Bombs must be something like that—a flash of light followed by the noise of the explosion. We were all arranged in alphabetical order so I couldn't sit with Angelica. She was two rows in

front of me—not close enough for holding hands. She
turned and smiled.

Preacher Ralston would have gone on forever had
the rain not broken him off. I think I got my diploma
on the run as I raced off the grandstand and sought
refuge under the old band shell. There were a lot of
hugs and kisses, but the rain had stopped when I
finally caught up to Angelica, and we spent a long
time just holding on to each other. I noticed even
Hack was pretty emotional. Tomorrow, we would all
be signing up for the draft. How do you train men to
aim a gun and kill?

I don't remember much of that night except that I
spent most of it with Angelica. We all headed out to
the dance hall and the sound of Roy's combo. The soft
lights were kind to the aging structure. I never let go
of Angelica until after signoff. Andy and Hack
seemed to want to be alone, too, so I didn't bother
them. We were all thinking about tomorrow and reg-
istering for the draft. You went from a high school kid
to a man overnight.

It was past three a.m. when I said goodnight to
Angelica, and I knew if I survived the war we'd be
married. She seemed to know it too, and all of a sudden my life as a war kid ended. Within a day, the end
would also come to Nazi Germany.

A hot summer sun beat down on the long line of
graduates outside our post office the next morning.
The night had been downright unkind to some as they
squinted against the light. It was almost two hours
before I faced a tough sergeant and took my oath.

We were all given a package of papers, and train tickets. Proud, and scared, Hack, Andy, and I made our way home.

Mom served lunch out on the back porch that noon, and I felt like a visitor now. The white frame house was the same, the garden was there too, but I kept seeing myself as a guest, passing through. Next thing I knew was a yell from Mom as she burst from the kitchen and jerked me out of my chair. It was all over in Europe. As we headed back to the kitchen to listen to the radio, the church bells started ringing.

Our town went pretty wild that night, and even though I knew Dad was in the Pacific, I also knew he was coming home now. The Japs couldn't hold out much longer. I also felt Hack's hand on my shoulder and knew trouble was brewing.

Hack had saved almost four years' worth of firecrackers and had spent the afternoon stripping the black powder from the tubes. The cannon which stood in front of the post office as a Civil War memorial was about to break an eighty-year period of silence.

Andy and I watched as Hack packed a sandwich bag filled with powder down the bore with the help of someone's clothes pole. Several issues of our local newspaper followed, and Hack finished the job by jamming a long, homemade fuse in the touch hole. It seemed like an eternity once I returned to the dance pavilion with Angelica until Hack's masterpiece let loose.

I'd never heard anything like that explosion in my life. The band, everyone, stopped, as dense smoke mixed with falling leaves filled the air. What we didn't hear was the sound of glass falling from the shattered windows in the post office. The smoke cleared, the band picked up the beat, and the sheriff dispatched two of his lieutenants to sweep up the broken glass. When I went to get the mail next morning, the post office had a plywood front, and the bore of the cannon was filled with fresh cement.

Epilogue

The war ended just in time for most of us to avoid being drafted. Ma knew from Pa's letters that something big was going to happen that summer of 1945. The big thing was something called an atomic bomb, dropped on Hiroshima August 6, 1945. Pa got home in September, and after being without a father for over four years, I first looked at him as a stranger. We had all changed, and it would take time for us to come together again as a family. Pa never told me much about the war, and I did not feel comfortable asking questions, either. In fact, it was not until he died almost thirty years after the war ended that Ma told of all the medals he had received. He was buried with full military honors in our town cemetery.

Andy and I became partners in his dad's machine shop after he retired. We now make electronic printed circuit boards instead of repairing machinery. Everything seems to be computer controlled now. Angelica went out east after high school graduation to college and majored in theater. We kept in contact with many letters, and after graduation she had a brief career acting off Broadway. I finally convinced her to come back, and Angelica and I were married two years after I finished at the university. Our three daughters are now in college, which has given Angelica time to become involved in our community theater.

Hack pretty much disappeared from sight, and about all that we knew was that he was running a string of companies worldwide. He did return for our twentieth high school reunion, and his private jet caused quite a stir at our local airport. Along the way, he had acquired a blonde companion who looked like she had just walked out of the pages of a girlie magazine. We were told later that Hack picked up the bill for the entire reunion party and dance. On the basis of money earned, Hack is our most successful classmate.

Our Japanese American friend Jimmey returned with his parents to San Francisco after the war. His parents wanted to be with many of their friends who had been released from the internment camps. I think it was about ten years after the war ended that Jimmey returned with his wife to teach math in our high school. He told me that his roots were now in our town, which I felt was a fine compliment. The kids say that he is a fantastic teacher.

My dog Bill began a new career as Pa's hunting companion. Some of Pa's friends laughed at Bill at first, but their laughter soon turned to envy as Bill flushed and fielded birds as well as any purebred. Bill always slept at the foot of my bed even while I was away. Bill died in his sleep one night while I was in Korea. Pa made a wood coffin for him, and Bill was buried with a small American flag draped over the coffin as befitted a K-9 veteran. He wore his official collar to his rest under the old hickory tree in our backyard. There was even an obituary line in the local paper about his passing.

The days of the great war are in the past now. But each year, on Memorial Day, Ma, Angelica, and I drive out to the old town cemetery overlooking the beautiful river bottomland. The marsh flowers are in full bloom at that time, and we place our own flowers at the foot of Pa's grave along with a small flag. I always felt that the war years foreshortened his life with us.

There are newer stones now, white against the green grass. Stones that mark the final resting places of men and women who served in Korea and Vietnam. My prayer is always the same that day as we walk from Pa's grave: please dear God, let there be no more war.

For other titles of related interest, write for our *free* catalog. Send your request to:

Galde Press, Inc.
PO Box 460
Lakeville MN 55044